THE
BIRTHDAY PRESENT 2050

THE
BIRTHDAY PRESENT
2050

WRITTEN BY **TANIA WISBAR**

DIRECTOR'S NOTE

Although we may describe this play as taking place in the future, it is a near future we are speaking of. The world has not changed so much technologically that we wouldn't recognize it. And our human feelings are much as they are today. But we are dealing with a social reality in which famine and disease are eliminated as well as poverty as we know it. The stasis of life is handled by the state and the continuation of life on an individual level is up to each individual, just like the management of one's bank account today is up to each of us. Thus, some of us are frugal and save, and others can't seem to keep their bankbooks in balance.

The one key difference in this world is that anything that has no use cannot afford to be kept, including people.

In this world of no homelessness or crime, there is also no disease. The only pills taken by anyone would be to end a life. And the worst offense in society is to remember the past prior to the institution of the new world order.

Old memories can only lead to dissatisfaction and can create tension that is not productive to a functioning society. As such, all past images, photos, and keepsakes are forbidden. Paintings and other images that refer to a past time are also not allowed.

As soon as the last elder who was born prior to the new times has died, all artifacts of that person must also be destroyed... so that the dishes from Felix's mother are only allowed to be kept as long as the eldest family member, Teresa, is alive.

'Video specs', 'e-letts', 'streaming', etc. are all terms used for public and personal communication. And the walls really do have ears; they also have emotions and can change color depending on the temperament of the conversations within.

A government big enough to give you everything you want, is a government big enough to take away everything you have.

**from left: GUY (Jeffrey Doornbos), TRINKA (Cheyenne Haynes)
and MARSHA (Elyssa Davalos)**

cover art by Nancy Nimoy
photo by Andrew Langholf
set by Kis Knekt

An Argyle Road Production

THE BIRTHDAY PRESENT 2050

WRITTEN BY TANIA WISBAR
DIRECTED BY JONATHAN SANGER

CAST

in order of appearance

TERESA HALLICK .... Salome Jens

MARSHA HALLICK ROMERO ....Elyssa Davalos

GUY.. Jeffrey Doornbos

TRINKA HALLICK ROMERO ....Cheyenne Haynes

SECURITY JAMES.. Demetrius Grosse

DOTTIE SYLVESTER* .... Jossara Jinaro

....Alexis De La Rocha

FELIX ROMERO HALLICK .... Juan Carlos Cantu

AUNT HELENE HALLICK JEFFERSON ....Katrina Lenk

UNCLE HARRY JEFFERSON HALLICK* ....James Black

.............................Antonio Charity

AUNT GLADYS HALLICK ....Janet Hoskins

*these roles double cast

This play was first performed at the Skylight Theater
in Los Angeles, California on March 19, 2011.

THE BIRTHDAY PRESENT 2050

A play in three scenes

by

Tania Wisbar

CAST OF CHARACTERS

TERESA HALLICK
Anglo, 72 years old. MARSHA'S mother.

MARSHA HALLICK ROMERO
Anglo, 48 years old.

FELIX ROMERO HALLICK
Hispanic, 48 years old. MARSHA'S husband.

TRINKA HALLICK ROMERO
Hispanic/American, 15 years old. Their daughter.

AUNT GLADYS HALLICK
Anglo, 50 years old. MARSHA's sister.

AUNT HELENE HALLICK JEFFERSON
Anglo, 43 years old. MARSHA'S sister.

UNCLE HARRY JEFFERSON HALLICK
African/American, mid-forties. HELENE'S husband.

AUNT SONIA HALLICK
Anglo, 38 years old. MARSHA'S sister. Only seen on a video spec.

GUY
Anglo, mid-thirties. Family coach.

DOTTIE SYLVESTER
Hispanic, 29 years old.

SECURITY JAMES
African/American, 35 years old.

SETTING
A high-rise condo.

TIME
Soon. Teresa's 72nd birthday.
The entire play takes place in one evening.

PRELUDE ONE

MUSIC: TERESA'S theme.

SETTING: Dead Center Stage is a small makeup table at which TERESA sits studying her reflection. TERESA sits in a wheelchair looking into the large oval mirror. The stage is in total darkness except for a stream of light that hits the mirror, bouncing on the surfaces of the other neighboring silhouetted windows so the audience sees TERESA'S image in several places and in several dimensions on the otherwise dark stage.

TERESA

I, Teresa Hallick, dress now for my birthday, my 72nd, the oldest person in this city of cold spaces.

I dress now in my tired black gown, fit for an old widowed woman, the last in this stony place of no color or flowers; birds do not come to rest on my window sill; dogs just a touch memory of warm eyes, gentle eyes and loyal welcome.

I dress now ready to feign surprise at what my daughters will do to keep me another year. Or not; not is fine with me; my memories hurt them, burden me.

I long for the arms of love my daughters took from me, out of love for me, not enough points left for their father. His name forever entombed in silent neglect.

They took my love, mirror to my ageing wrinkled self; they took my awakening joy of being another's self and left me this stony shelf of half life.

I dress now, old black gown, long dark shawl in which I can hide from my daughters, from myself as they quarrel among themselves, quarrel in outloud words and seething bitterness. To keep me will cost.

TERESA (CONT.)

I know them so well; each will bring a present of points...will they be enough to keep me another year? Two years ago they took love from me. With that I was left to drift in time, which will end tonight, or next year.

I am ready now. I wait. Security James will come to pick me up and take me to Marsha's place...I am prepared to travel now. I have seen this before.

    MUSIC: fades out.

SCENE ONE

SETTING. A first floor living room with a kitchen area stage right. A large dining table occupies the center of the stage with a half dozen chairs around it. The fine old china, plates, bowls, silverware and lace napkins are on the table. There's a short, barely visible flight of stairs leading upstage left to a small but visible bedroom. A large frame covers the living room's upstage "Wall" and, unless there is a special governmental bulletin, it has an abstract, unobtrusive design. Behind the monitor there is a wall behind which actors can pass going from one side of the stage and reappearing at the other. Stage left there's a door leading to a hallway and at an angle downstage right is the front door.

MARSHA gives the appearance of being controlled but nervous laughter often fills an otherwise silent moment. She has two old curlers in her bangs.

MARSHA looks disdainfully at an elongated box and places it on the kitchen floor. She speaks into the stove:

MARSHA

In 45 minutes cook for 90 seconds.

She moves quickly to the long, festive dining table.

MARSHA is beginning to set the table. She counts the napkins while humming tunelessly.

MARSHA

Nine plates, napkins, cups, glasses for drinks....

The Wall monitor lights up. A man's smiling face appears on the screen. It is "GUY". He is dressed in a blue jacket.

GUY

Hello...

MARSHA, who has had her back to the monitor, jumps with surprise and turns to it.

MARSHA

Oh! Oh dear! What a surprise.

GUY

I did not mean to startle you. Let me introduce myself. My name is "Guy". I will be your coach.

> *MARSHA quickly takes off her curlers and shakes out her hair.*

MARSHA

My name is Marsha Hallick Romero.

GUY

What kind of coach would I be if I did not know that? We wanted to make sure you received our flowers. With them we become part of this celebration for your mother's landmark birthday.

MARSHA

How nice of you. Yes, the flowers are here... but...

> *She edges quickly towards the kitchen to retrieve the box she had earlier dismissively put on the floor and places it on the table.*

GUY

Is there a problem? I am your coach. Here to help you. What do you need?

MARSHA

(nervously)

I didn't know the new system already worked.

GUY

You answered the census. Thank you for that. When I saw your family name I was deeply gratified that you chose to be part of phase one. This is a historic reaching out by The Committee to bring us more closely into your lives. We are in the testing phase. We want to make sure we are sensitive to you in everything we do. Now, how can I help you?

> *She opens the box hurriedly.*

MARSHA

The flowers... how do they open?

GUY

Do you see the instructions that came with the flowers?

She looks at an instruction sheet.

MARSHA

Hmmmmm. These, I think are in, well, maybe in Chinese.

She is turning them upside down. Finally she holds up the instructions so GUY can see that they really are in Chinese.

GUY

Oh my. We tried so hard to get each family's language correctly identified. Even the fringe tribes. I will have to file a departmental complaint.

(pause)

Do you see a little lever at the bottom of each stem?

MARSHA runs her fingers along the stem and finds the lever.

MARSHA

Here it is.

GUY

Gently slide it up.

MARSHA does and an insta-flower pops out of the surrounding green feathers.

MARSHA

(looking astonished)

How amazing... an insta-flower with feathers. A brand new kind of flower. How nice. And surprising.

GUY

We also provided a special vase. Please use it. I chose it myself.

She brushes a feather from off her nose.

MARSHA

How thoughtful. A vase. And so useful.

She put the stems into the vase haphazardly.

GUY

I see on my system that your daughter is almost at your door. I will leave you to greet her in private. It was lovely meeting you. May I call you "Marsha"? Or would you prefer a more formal salutation?

MARSHA

Marsha is fine. May I call you "Guy"?

GUY

Please do. Remember I am always here to help you.

MARSHA

Thank you.

GUY

Goodbye, Marsha. Have a lovely party.

MARSHA

Goodbye, Guy.

A red light goes on at the top of the door. The monitor goes blank.

SECURITY JAMES (O.S.)

HERE! Here we are.

The automatic door opens with a whooshing noise. TRINKA and SECURITY JAMES enter, cross the threshold and the door whooshes shut behind them.

MARSHA rushes to the door. TRINKA, bright-eyed and dressed in a light white traveling uniform, is accompanied by SECURITY JAMES, a handsome, quiet-spoken man. He stands in the doorway adjusting what looks almost like a uniform made of soft fabric. TRINKA enters. Mother and daughter's hugs and kisses overlap.

MARSHA

Trinka, my darling Trinka.

TRINKA

Mama! Mama! I'm home. Mama! Mama! I'm home.

MARSHA and TRINKA hold each other. TRINKA twists out of her mother's arms, dashes across the stage and runs into her bedroom, looks it over, quickly opens her backpack, pulls out a round globe, hides it under the bed pillow, puts the empty backpack on the floor and rushes back to SECURITY JAMES and her mother.

MARSHA

Oh, Trinka! You're here!

She gives TRINKA a quick hug.

Oh, Security James, we missed you last year. You usually bring my treasure home to me. Where were you?

She takes his hand.

Come in, come in. Let me get you something to eat, to drink. Please come in! I'm so grateful to you.

He hesitates at the door.

SECURITY JAMES

It was a long journey, but...

TRINKA pulls him around the table.

TRINKA

Wait 'til you see the feast for my grandmother's birthday! Remember how beautiful it always is?

> *SECURITY JAMES smiles and enters the room. He gasps as he sees the table. TRINKA pulls him excitedly around the table, obviously very proud. Wandering around it, SECURITY JAMES touches a dish, a flower.*

SECURITY JAMES

Yes, it is beautiful! Your mother will be pleased. She's 71 this birthday, isn't she?

MARSHA

(uneasy)

No, 72.

SECURITY JAMES

Of course she is. I missed being with you last year.

MARSHA

Where were you?

SECURITY JAMES

(exuberant)

I was sent for a period of reorientation. What a wonderful experience; to learn again how important my work is.

> *He snaps back into the present and studies the festive table.*

I remember this now. You do so much to make it pretty...

TRINKA

Do you have a table like that for your grandmother?

SECURITY JAMES

No.

TRINKA

Oh.

SECURITY JAMES

I don't have a grandmother, anymore.

TRINKA

Of course you don't. She would have been too old.

MARSHA

Trinka, I think you should go change your clothes.

TRINKA turns away.

TRINKA

I'm going!

She stops and turns back to SECURITY JAMES as she walks towards the hallway behind her bedroom.

Was your mother also too old?

SECURITY JAMES

(abruptly)

Yes. I had no brothers, no sisters. There was only me. I couldn't... I didn't have enough-------

MARSHA

Trinka, go—go right now!

TRINKA runs down the hallway ostensibly behind her bedroom.

The young, they don't always understand.

MARSHA crosses to SECURITY JAMES. She tries to calm him.

SECURITY JAMES

(empowered)

I enlisted to be a Global Soldier. They pay me well. Benefits are good; on top of the 750 points almost everyone else gets Securities earn an extra 250 points a year that are put into an account for when we are older.

(beat, in his mind he is remembering the "drill")

You see we can't join if we have family. We must be free of all ties or we couldn't do our jobs.

MARSHA

I don't think I understand.

> *SECURITY JAMES laughs, then moves in close to MARSHA and speaks softly.*

SECURITY JAMES

People confess to us what they did to get enough points. We're like high priests. Sometimes, they even try to borrow a few.

MARSHA

Did you ever...?

SECURITY JAMES

Oh, no! The extra 250 points has to be accounted for all the time, or we lose our jobs... Sometimes, people even ask me to make the decision for them.

MARSHA

Do you?

SECURITY JAMES

No, I couldn't do that. I just listen.

> *LIGHTS come up on TRINKA in her bedroom sitting on her bed. She has changed offstage and is now wearing a simple blouse and skirt with a pocket in it.*

> *The LIGHTS go down on TRINKA and come back on MARSHA and SECURITY JAMES.*

MARSHA

I guess that's the way the world is.

SECURITY JAMES

Your daughter is beginning to understand. She's a good girl. She even took a job outside to earn a few more points. She worries about you and her father. How old is he?

MARSHA

We're the same age, 48.

(laughing uneasily)

We have some years before she has to worry... we try to save.

SECURITY JAMES

With your mother, that must be hard. You should have had more than one child.

MARSHA

No, I asked for a baby girl.

SECURITY JAMES

You didn't take State Assignment? How strange!

MARSHA

I didn't want to take the chance of not having a little girl.

SECURITY JAMES

Everyone else takes the two assigned... for later. It can make all the difference.

MARSHA haphazardly fixes SECURITY JAMES a snack and a drink.

MARSHA

The system found Felix for me. It was not easy to find a man who would agree to be limited to just one child. But Felix did, and we got our miracle; my Trinka.

She hands him thedrink and snack.

Everything's fine. I like the way things are. The social point system helps us. And you bring Trinka to me. Here, rest a while.

She offers him a chair.

DOTTIE enters, flying through the door, it makes the whooshing sound as it opens and shuts behind her. She's a pretty woman, bursting with energy, and talking in a barrage.

DOTTIE

You forgot to turn off the green. Here, let me.

> *She pushes an invisible button by the door. The light above the door that had been green, now goes to red.*

You always forget, Marsha! Someday, I'll hear you yelling for help. If you aren't more careful you're going to be put on the watch list. Where are the presents going? I brought mine early.

> *She pulls out a small, flat, ornately wrapped package.*

Marsha, the table's beautiful! Oh, to have such lovely things! Felix's mother had such beautiful dishes. I am so used to seeing them at the birthdays. The things in the old days were made better, weren't they? It will be sad when your mother is gone They will be gone also. Now, I brought four; that's all I could spare. Maybe your mama can buy herself a treat—maybe go to a concert, or a new dress. It's a bonus, since you have enough points—you do, don't you?

> (adding up very clearly)

You and Felix saved 400; Sonia and Gladys have 250. Helene and Harry, the cheapskates, have 100. That's 750. That's enough, isn't it?

MARSHA

Dottie, you're a marvel. Yes, we have enough.

> *MARSHA takes the package and places it on the small side table that sits near the dining table.*

You really shouldn't have, Dottie. Four is really a very large gift. Are you sure?

DOTTIE

Where's Trinka? I heard her voice.

MARSHA

Changing. She's so grown-up, so beautiful.

> *DOTTIE spots SECURITY JAMES. She crosses to him practically oozing feminine, flirtatious charm. She holds out her hand to shake his hand. SECURITY JAMES stands up.*

DOTTIE

Security James! How nice to see you again! You look maaarvellous!

MARSHA

Dottie, we have enough points. You keep yours for yourself.

> *She extends the flat package toward DOTTIE who crosses back towards MARSHA, hesitates for a moment then accepts it.*

DOTTIE

I could put them in my Life Account—are you sure?

MARSHA

Quite sure.

DOTTIE

I'd like to bring your mother something.

> *MARSHA hugs DOTTIE.*

MARSHA

She'll be so pleased you're here for her party! Just you without anything will make her happy.

DOTTIE

I want to bring something. She's always treated me as one of her girls. Here I go on an endless quest for some shining gift—

> *Leaving, she calls back to SECURITY JAMES:*

It was nice seeing you!

> *She exits, hitting the button by the door so the light goes from red to green, the door whooshes open and she exits, smiling at SECURITY JAMES.*

SECURITY JAMES

Whew, if I had her energy, I'd be a chief of my section. I've got to go, too. Thanks for the snack.

> *MARSHA crosses toward TRINKA'S room.*

MARSHA
(looking worriedly towards Trinka's room)

You're more than welcome... What in the world is keeping Trinka? She should come say "thank you".

SECURITY JAMES

Ah kids... You shouldn't worry too much about Trinka. I see so many kids in my job. Some of them—only a few—become problems for us dealing in forbidden memory disks, old photos... I give them one warning. Give them a little room and they get over it. Kids – don't worry so much.

MARSHA

There's no trouble, is there? You didn't hear anything? I wouldn't want not to know.

SECURITY JAMES

No, there's no trouble. I'd tell you if I knew. Trinka does well in school, very well.

MARSHA
(laughing nervously)

Mothers! We all worry, don't we, Security James? You must see it all the time.

(beat)

I see so little of her, now that she's away at school... only on the elders' birthdays. And now there's only one.

SECURITY JAMES

Yes, it's a pity that your father is no longer here. That must have been a difficult choice. I was told his passing was peaceful. The pills worked quickly.

MARSHA
(looking away)

Yes, that was... yes.

SECURITY JAMES

I am sure you miss the extra visit. But we do send you Trinka's folder summary every three months. You do get it, don't you?

MARSHA

She's my child! In the video specs, she always looks so small, so alone. They make me feel worse.

SECURITY JAMES

Should I put in a cancel order for the specs?

MARSHA

No! Oh, no, please!

She stops. She takes a breath.

Maybe, you could get her to smile a little more.

SECURITY JAMES

You were brought up when children were kept at home, weren't you?

MARSHA

Yes.

SECURITY JAMES smiles and shrugs. He picks up his jacket.

SECURITY JAMES

Mother Hallick, this is the only system I have ever known. It's the best. An excellent system. No more crime or violence. No disease. Everybody's protected; all work for each other. Everyone has a place to live, food. I remember stories from my grandmother—funny stories.

(becoming the cheerleader)

How could people live like that? No one to take care of anyone. This is a good system. Now we're all responsible! Imagine! Old people just left somewhere… anywhere. This is better. And it's better for the young, too. The system protects them from wandering around alone. My grandmother told me both parents had to work back then, just to try to make it, never could catch up.

Moving into SECURITY JAMES, she speaks quietly:

MARSHA

When they changed the system… my mother protested.

SECURITY JAMES

I know, she became a legend. One of the most famous stories from that time. None of us understand it.

MARSHA turns away, hiding from his words.

MARSHA

But this way, is it better? Is it better to make a family decide every year?

SECURITY JAMES

Look at it this way; somebody wants something. Like a gold bracelet from the Exchange. That uses up points—nobody says out loud that a decision was made, but at birthday time there are suddenly not enough points.

MARSHA

Meaning?

SECURITY JAMES

It's in the system. We can tell about three months before the birthday what each family member has saved… if there's going to be enough… if they're going to make it. Families know how to count but sometimes they'd just rather not. We make contingency plans either way.

MARSHA

What if there's an emergency? What if a child gets into trouble? What if a family uses their points to help?

SECURITY JAMES

Then that's the decision, isn't it? Nobody has to spell it out. Well, I've got to go get your mother. She has another year.

He crosses to the door.

Congratulations to all of you. Don't worry so, Mother Hallick.

He pushes the door button, it opens and he exits, the door closing behind him.

MARSHA crosses to the kitchen and returns to finish the table. She forgets something and goes into the kitchen.

MARSHA

Trinka, darling, can you come down?

The LIGHTS become brighter in TRINKA'S room. TRINKA is visible taking the disk, actually a silver globe, from under her pillow and studies it, very uncertain what to do, then decides to quickly put it into a disk player by her bed. The player is round with a carved out center into which the silver globe fits. TRINKA'S back is to the audience but her posture shows fear. MUSIC: "Video Green" plays with video. The audience can see the images. The Wall fills with a picture of a young woman walking through a forested area, carrying many flowers and leading a small dog, a sequence that will end with the woman and dog on the ground in a small clearing.

MARSHA looks up the stairs for a moment then goes into the kitchen and aimlessly moves things around..

Trinka, darling, could you come down, please?

TERESA (VOICE OVER - REMOTE)

I see you now sitting, watching the illegal pictures of the past. Be careful, Trinka, you must be careful. Must not get caught, or the one who passed the disk to you...I was young then, I did not know so long ago that I would bring such harm across the years to today. Go to your mother, she is calling you. Go to her. The pictures are from another time. Be careful, my beautiful grandchild.

TRINKA quickly removes the disk and hides it again under her pillow. MUSIC fades.

TRINKA

Yes, Mama.

She comes running into the room. They hug. MARSHA touches TRINKA'S face.

MARSHA

I haven't even had a good look at you. You look so grown up. Turn around let me see you. Darling, what is it? You've been crying!

TRINKA

Nothing, Mama; it's nothing.

>   *MARSHA pulls out two chairs from the table and sitting in one, she indicates that TRINKA is to sit in the other.*

MARSHA

Please tell me. There's so little I can do for you... but I can listen—

TRINKA

There was a boy...

MARSHA

(alarmed)

At school?

>   *They look at each other. Fear shows in MARSHA'S face; she turns away, hiding.*

Not at school, then? At the job? Security James said you even got a job.

TRINKA

Yes. Everyone knew I was going home for Grandmother's birthday but the boy wanted to ask me about her... I think he liked me; he touched my face.

MARSHA

And?

TRINKA

Nothing.

MARSHA

Nothing? No points taken away?

TRINKA

No.

MARSHA

Are you sure?

TRINKA

(beat , she is not telling the truth)

He gave me......

(she hesitates, changes her mind)

Later he sent me a telenote.

MARSHA

Trinka, you're very important to them. Because of Grandmother, you're special. They want you to have a good profession... but they also watch us closer because of Grandmother. You'll be paired with a boy chosen for you from the correct pool.

TRINKA

I may not like that. Did Grandmother get to choose?

MARSHA

In the old days things were different. Now... well, pairing is engineered along specific guidelines.

TRINKA

All this year I waited to see Grandmother. I remember when I was little she would tell me stories. She would hold me close and whisper in my ear of another world...

MARSHA

Did you believe the stories...? She could have just been making them up.

TRINKA

Maybe... but she would draw little pictures of things she said existed then. I know she believed them. Could I have chosen a boy to love? Were her stories real, Mama?

MARSHA

I really do not know what she told you...

TRINKA

She said there was a time without points... Why were the old ways taken away? She wouldn't tell me. She said I was too young... that you would tell me. Mama, I am old enough now, tell me.

MARSHA

Darling, not now. There is no time now. We have to finish setting the table. Why don't we do that?

TRINKA

I want to know what happened. Why were the old ways taken away?

MARSHA fusses with the table, wandering to the buffet and back. Seeming lost in thought, she absently picks up plates then puts them down.

MARSHA

It didn't seem important. At first it just seemed strange. The little girl standing alone in the schoolyard in the cold. She had no shoes. We had never seen that.

TRINKA

A child without shoes.

TRINKA stands confused, amazed.

What does that have to do with Grandmother?

MARSHA

We really don't have time. Your father will be here any moment.

She continues to fuss with the table.

TRINKA

Yes, we do. I have to know. What happened to the little girl?

MARSHA

They came to get her. Trinka, the forks are missing. Please get the forks.

TRINKA

What about the little g...?

> *Throughout this speech MARSHA is drawn increasingly into her memories although she struggles not to be overcome by them.*

MARSHA

They built...

> (pause)

A few weeks later, a very large stadium, to hold thousands of seats. And then another one, and next to that one, a third. It seemed to go very quickly while we watched. From every seat you could see into the others. And there were giant monitors everywhere. One day we were all ordered to go to the stadiums; each family together, and each in seats reserved for us. When each stadium was full, the gates were closed. They began to bring in the children who had no shoes... hundreds of children came silently into the center.

TRINKA

How old were they?

MARSHA

Little ones, bigger ones... maybe the oldest was 10.

TRINKA

Where did they come from?

MARSHA

We never knew. We sat and looked at the children. They looked at the ground.

> *MARSHA begins to cry.*

MARSHA wipes away her tears.

MARSHA (CONT.)

We were told to have one child from each family go down, take off their shoes and put them on one of the children in the center.

TRINKA

Who went from our family?

MARSHA

Your Aunt Sonia. She was just the same age as the little girl.

TRINKA

Who did Aunt Sonia give her shoes to?

MARSHA

A little boy. She just chose him.

TRINKA

What was in the other stadium?

MARSHA

They brought in all the people who lived in the alleys and doorways. Every family in THAT stadium had to bring a blanket.

TRINKA

Who gave the doorway people their blankets?

MARSHA

The eldest from each family. They would go down and wrap their blankets around one of the alley people. For seven days we looked at the children; looked at the people clutching their blankets, and then the stadiums became colder. At first people talked, children played, babies cried, people began to argue, families fought. And then people began to turn on their neighbors. After four days nobody spoke or fought anymore. At the end of seven days, we were thanked for our service and allowed to go home.

TRINKA

What happened to the children, the blanket people?

TRINKA is clearly getting impatient with her mother.

MARSHA

I don't know. We never learned about most of them.

TRINKA

There must be a way of finding out...

MARSHA

No, it is better to leave it alone. Perhaps we didn't need to know.

She abruptly begins to cross to the kitchen, changes her mind and walks outside of the audiences' view down the "hall" behind the wall monitor.

TRINKA

Well I want to know.

GUY'S smiling face appears. TRINKA jumps surprised.

Who are you?

GUY

Oh... I see... Your mother forgot to tell you about me. I understand. You, too, have been very busy since you got home... My that is a very nice outfit you have on. I myself am very interested in fashion... very responsible actually, along with the rest of the design committee, in choosing that lovely travel outfit you arrived in.

He beams happily at the memory.

TRINKA

(very impatient)

Who are you and what are you doing here?

GUY

I am the family's new coach... now what can I do for you? Trinka. You're Trinka. I know that. You are more attractive than your file photo.

> *TRINKA is half charmed.*

TRINKA

I was wondering if you have some old streams of the stadiums?

> *MARSHA reenters the room from "the hall". She looks stricken as she sees GUY'S face on the monitor interacting with TRINKA.*

GUY

Of course we keep the official record... how else would we remember how we all became one large community?

TRINKA

Can you send them?

MARSHA

There is no time. They will be here any minute.

> *GUY looks at a different screen and comes back to them smiling benignly.*

GUY

Actually, they are running late... Isn't that just like a family? But there is just enough time for the Stadium record. So, Marsha, your permission?

> (he turns his eyes to TRINKA)

Mothers always know best, don't ever forget that.

> *MARSHA is visibly shaken.*

TRINKA

You have to let me see them.

MARSHA

(almost in tears)

All right...

MUSIC: "The Stadium" begins over the images of the shoeless children.

The Wall hums while GUY'S face fades and is replaced by an image of a large, cold stadium. Only children's feet are seen struggling into worn shoes. Hundreds of little feet.

That image is replaced by another stadium showing stooped shoulders being covered by blankets; no faces, just hands are shown covering the shoulders.

TERESA (VOICE OVER-REMOTE)

The children came from all corners of neglect, from living in empty parks, some in cars, left to form packs of hunger, often running past ambitions we needed to keep. The children, the children, tiny, a few bigger, hands held, sheltering the smaller ones against the biting wind, sweeping through this treacherous man-built warren of a space, we were made to witness our disgrace.

I clutched my own, turned my back, I was not brave. My youngest slipped out of my grasp, down the stadium steps, tripping as she took off her shoes, laughing with joy, running pell-mell to become lost in that drifting space of little children, giving her shoes away as I screamed her name. Sonia!!!!!.

MUSIC fades and voice fades.

GUY

These are the official records. What a wonderful week it was.

MARSHA

(fighting for self control)

Thank you, Guy... I really need you to leave.

GUY

We do have one more stadium.

MARSHA

No, thank you. This is enough!

> *GUY purses his lips and looks disapproving.*

GUY

Well, if you insist... I can be sensitive to your needs.

> *He fades and the Wall goes dark.*

TRINKA

What happened next?

MARSHA

For several months every night the pictures were beamed into everyone's home. At the next election we were asked to approve the point system.

TRINKA

How old were you, Mama?

MARSHA

I was your age, 15.

TRINKA

So you remember the time before the stadiums...

MARSHA

Not always that clearly—we never spoke about those times again.

TRINKA

What was in the last stadium? And what does it have to do with Grandmother? Tell me!

> *The door lights up green as FELIX, a soft-shouldered, outwardly ebullient but nervous man, enters the room smiling.*

FELIX

There she is.

> *TRINKA throws herself at FELIX. He lifts her high in the air and swings her around.*

My little beauty!!!

TRINKA

(laughing)

Papa! Put me down! I'm too big to lift!

> *FELIX puts TRINKA down and studies her closely.*

FELIX

Not too big... but maybe too grown up. From now on, I'll only kiss you on each cheek.

> *He does so, giving her exaggerated kisses. TRINKA starts to giggle. MARSHA looks on pleased. Lights flash on the door in a signaling pattern.*

They're on their way up. I'll go wash! Don't go away!

> *FELIX exits to the hallway.*

MARSHA

Your aunts! They're on their way up!

TRINKA

They'll go anywhere for a free meal.

MARSHA

What did you say?

TRINKA

It's freeloader's time! They'll come to eat; some won't come, of course. Not my dumb cousins. They always stay away—too busy! Too scared is what it is! Afraid they'll be seen with Grandmother!

MARSHA

Trinka, they're your own family!

TRINKA

But not Grandmother's family. The legend she is, is too much for them. Grandmother has never been to Aunt Helene's house! Too risky! And too expensive! I'm learning the system. I know that Grandmother gets most of her points from you and Daddy... I did lose points. 5.

> *MARSHA puts her hands over her face for a few seconds then looks up.*

MARSHA

Was it the boy? Was it the telenote?

> *TRINKA nods.*

TRINKA

Yes. He had beautiful eyes with a curtain of lashes.

MARSHA

Security James said there was no trouble! Said you'd even gotten a job to earn some extra points!

TRINKA

He doesn't know. They said if I admitted I had made a mistake and gave up the points it would not be on my record... You still haven't told me what Grandmother's story has to do with the doorway people and the children. Now I only see her once a year! Maybe the stories she told me were real. That world must have been beautiful. Before the point system.

MARSHA

(sighing)

Yes, in some ways. But it was also very hard, I remember. There were too many loves to take care of, and never enough money to do it. The social point system keeps Grandmother with us in a way. You really can't look back, Trinka; you mustn't.

Pause. She kneels next to TRINKA'S chair.

MARSHA (CONT.)

Sometimes when I watch a spec of you from school, I so much want to touch you. I read all your eletts over and over, can't wait the year to see you again, see how you've grown, changed. A spec every three months just isn't enough to keep up with you.

She laughs.

I even asked Security James to get you to smile when the specs are made.

TRINKA

Have I changed that much? I can't wait to see Grandmother. How much has she changed?

Lights flash on the door.

FELIX re-enters from the hallway.

MARSHA

They're here. Trinka. Be nice. It's Grandmother's birthday again. We're all together.

FELIX embraces Marsha affectionately.

FELIX

The table looks beautiful. Like you my love. It's going to be a fine party.

MARSHA embraces her daughter and husband and leads them to the door.

They're here. Our family is here.

LIGHTS go down. Curtain falls.

PRELUDE TWO

MUSIC: TERESA'S theme.

SETTING: In a far right corner of the dark stage, TERESA sits in her wheel chair. SECURITY JAMES standing behind her, holding on to the chair's handles to secure her. Lights flash in rapid and fragmented patterns across TERESA'S and JAMES'S faces. It has the effect of their moving rapidly.

TERESA

We travel now, Security James with me, fleeting shadows of tall buildings hurtle past, throw our faces into twilight, night – scattered- neon momentary light dancing over our shrouded selves.

Security James, assigned to me as I became 65, we do not ask, answer or even speak of that night two years ago as my love and I, holding hands, thinking all was well, took this same journey that I now take to find my fate. Security James was there as the points fell short, as they took my love away, the only arms that had ever protected me. James too turned around to face the monitor, uttered no regret. My daughters held me back; I could not go, was forbidden to tear at my hair, and shout the house down.

James, my Security, my jailer, my friend, does he wonder if tonight will be my end?
What will my daughters and their husbands decide?
Marsha, my second daughter will cry, that's what seconds do;
Sonia, my youngest will seek a fight;
Helene will already have counted the jewelry she will buy if only I leave without a debate,
And Gladys, having loved her father, wonders if there is something about me that should survive, except silence.
There were no words for their father, my joyful love until death.
Only silence.
No place to weep.

MUSIC: TERESA'S theme fades out.

SCENE TWO

MUSIC: Light cocktail music plays.

The family cocktail party is in full swing. MARSHA is serving platters of hors d'oeuvres. FELIX is making and passing drinks; AUNT HELENE shows off her new dress. HARRY, with a drink in his hand and exaggerated posture, is doing a parody of ogling her. AUNT GLADYS is snitching tastes out of things on the insta-stove. She is constantly eating, which might explain her girth.

MUSIC ends.

TRINKA rearranges the insta-flowers on the dining table, then carefully removes each identical flat offering from the little table that holds the gifts, puts them on the dining table, picks up the little table, moves it to the center of the living room, retrieves the gifts, and places them back on the little table. MARSHA spots TRINKA.

MARSHA

Darling, what are you doing?

TRINKA

I want Grandmother to see them as soon as she comes in. That way, she won't have to worry.

MARSHA

Trinka, she already knows everything's all right.

TRINKA

Can I keep it here, please?

MARSHA

Of course, darling.

HELENE

You're becoming a little brood, Trinka. Come talk to your old auntie. Do you like my new dress? Are there any nice boys in your section at school?

FELIX

Leave her alone, Helene.

TRINKA

(straight-faced)

Nobody as nice as my cousins.

> *HELENE looks at her suspiciously. TRINKA dashes out of the room and down the "hallway" behind the Wall monitor.*
>
> *DOTTIE comes flying through the door, which makes the usual noise. DOTTIE looks up at the door light. She is holding a single, beautiful, real flower. To no one in particular she says:*

DOTTIE

What a family, you left the green on again. Oh, hello, everybody. Isn't this beautiful?! Just right for such a grand birthday. I made it to the Exchange just before it closed… actually it was the only flower they had.

> *HARRY takes the flower from DOTTIE. He smells its fragrance.*

HARRY

Long ago, they smelled like heaven. Teresa used to take Marsha and me as little kids to help her plant her garden. We would turn the earth and kiss the sunflowers, so long ago, Marsha, Teresa, and me. It was the happiest time in my life. I always thought we would be together…

> *HELENE turns away. HARRY, who is quite drunk, returns the flower to DOTTIE, then turns to the little table, picks up one of the flat packages, and pretends to smell it.*

With this kind of present, you can't smell it but you can say and really mean "I needed that".

HELENE

(forced laughter)

Isn't he clever?

HARRY waves the package at FELIX.

HARRY

Now, how many points are in this one? Felix, dear brother-in-law, how about a little bet? Is it 5 or 50? Or maybe more?

Throughout this scene GLADYS wanders from the kitchen to the living room always picking from the hors d'oeuvres plates she carries. She munches constantly and chews while saying:

GLADYS

It's a safe bet that the least amount is from you and Helene. Oh, dear. I didn't mean to say that.

(everybody looks embarrassed)

MARSHA

Dottie, I said a small gift. Mama will love it. Flowers mean so much to her, but you shouldn't have.

TRINKA, having heard DOTTIE'S voice, comes flying across the room and runs to hug DOTTIE. They twirl each other around.

TRINKA

Dottie, Dottie, you're marvelous. You always bring the best surprises.

DOTTIE

Trinka, look at you. Just look at you. You're all grown up. I saw your last spec but you're even more beautiful in person. Did you get my elett?

TRINKA

Yes, I'm sorry I didn't answer. I was…

DOTTIE

That's okay. You're like my little sister and my best little friend no matter what you do. Now, where should I put this?

TRINKA

Oh, here, right in the middle of the table. Then the table will be perfect. Won't Grandmother be surprised—a real flower.

>*HARRY stands.*

HARRY

Well, Felix, what do you think about the new car out?

FELIX

Which one?

HARRY

Which one? Which one? The one and only one. How many cars are there? One kind. You get your choice out of a choice of one.

HELENE

Isn't he clever?

HARRY

To buy or not to buy. That is the question.

HELENE

>(applauding)

Oh, Harry.

>*GLADYS exits to the kitchen.*

Next year—next year we're going to get a car.

HARRY

A car, Helene has decided to get a car!

>*Everything stops. The rest of the family looks at them stunned, except for GLADYS, who enters from the kitchen and mindlessly chirps in.*

GLADYS

If you're getting a car, I'm going to take a vacation or maybe go to a spa. With Mama gone, there will be so many more points...

> *TRINKA looks at her aunts with horror. She runs out of the room to her bedroom.*

> *MARSHA starts after her, then stops and turns on both her sisters angrily.*

MARSHA

(incoherent)

Is that all any of you think about? When Mama will be gone, life will be beautiful, easier, cars faster, vacation spots filled with romance. You all disgust me!

> *HELENE turns her back and plays with her necklace.*

HELENE

That's not fair. We've done our share. It's been seven years. Every year... We all pitch in to raise the 750 she needs each year.

GLADYS

I'm sorry, Marsha. Of course, you're right. We can't lose Mama too. I wasn't thinking.

HELENE

(turning on GLADYS)

You hypocrite! For years, you've talked about going on a vacation.

(to MARSHA)

She's not telling the truth!

FELIX

(trying to pull the group together but also tired of the wrangling)

When Mama reached 65, we all met and agreed we would keep her as long as possible. Helene, Harry, please. Your boys are grown now. Both have jobs, it should be easier for you now to give more.

MARSHA

Each year, Helene, you've welched a little more! You grudgingly give up a few points. Gladys gives more than you and she's alone! When was the last time you invited Mama to spend the weekend?

HELENE

Security James sees her on Sundays.

MARSHA

Why? Because Gladys and Sonia and I can't every Sunday. When we don't go see her, her Security does. And you, Helene, and your sons never go at all. Where, by the way, Harry, are your sons?

> *HELENE picks up one of the little wrapped presents and waves it at her family.*

HELENE

That does it! No matter what we do, it's not enough for you! I've kept an exact ledger all this time and we've done more than our share.

GLADYS

I go because I have no place else to go.

HELENE

This is the last year.

DOTTIE

Are you saying this is your Mama's last birthday?

HELENE

No, I'm saying-

> *She angrily waves the wrapped present.*

that this is our last contribution. I'm sure the rest of you will manage without our "small" gift.

> *FELIX tries to embrace her.*

FELIX

Helene, like you, I'm tired too. Of the extra job and never getting time off... and always worrying. But... please, without you, we may not be able to keep Mama.

HELENE

You won't understand, or even forgive the way I think, but Mama is already the oldest living parent in this city. Doesn't it ever occur to anyone else that maybe we've all done enough?

FELIX

Your mother is a legend, Helene.

HELENE

Which has brought all of us grief since we were children.

MARSHA

That's not true.

> *HELENE crosses to MARSHA angrily.*

HELENE

It is true. We've always been watched more carefully than anyone else, always had to do more and better. Marsha—you love Mama, Gladys and Sonia love Mama, I love Mama. What makes you think she is more special to you than to me?

> *MARSHA shakes HELENE and then abruptly lets her go, crossing away from her.*

MARSHA

(anger giving way to memory)

She is my memory. I need it. I need it alive and living through my mother. As long as I can see her, I can see places that once knew me, streets that felt my step. Through her I am once again a child without limits. Loving who I choose. I won't let your car destroy my mother.

> *GLADYS mindlessly munches and speaks in a monotone.*

GLADYS

I miss my father.

(accusing HELENE)

We lost him after you bought a house outside the city.

HELENE

(screaming at GLADYS)

How dare you!!!

GLADYS

(accusing all of them, each turns away)

He was my memory…. you never asked how it was; not one of you ever asked. Why did you not ask how it was at the end? Which one of you will go with Mama? Only I went with Papa. All alone, the two of us.

They all look at GLADYS as if she has broken a sacred trust. GLADYS starts with a list of complaints but is slowly drawn back into her memory of how their father died.

It was very quiet. Everything white, with a blue ceiling. A soft rain fell on us. I held him. I felt that he was smiling as he told me how much he loved me, the first of his children. He told me he wanted to close his eyes. The pills worked very quickly. Papa was gone. I wept over his body, touching his hair, kissing his still fingers, turned his hand so for one last time I could nuzzle my face into the soft inner palm as I had done so often as a child. When the attendants left the room, I rocked him in my arms. I took off the sheet to feel his body one last time, searching for the beat of his heart. The attendant came back to remove the blindfold from my eyes and I could see for myself that Papa was gone. They had me sign the paper.

MARSHA reaches towards her sister but GLADYS turns away.

He loved me the best. Nobody will ever love me again. You want to keep our mother, we have.

(to MARSHA and HELENE)

You have so much, all the prizes of what is left: a daughter, 2 sons, husbands. Each serves as a mirror to your soul, each a sound within the silence. I am alone, have no mirror, no fragment of light. I will live in forever silence.

HELENE

Don't blame me. You made the choice. None of us had anything to do with it. You signed the contract. You agreed you would be single in exchange for 10 extra years. Anyway, I couldn't go. I was busy. We were moving.

GLADYS

Would you have saved for me?

> *Her sisters and their husbands step away. GLADYS just looks at them then walks to stand behind the table.*

Nobody?

> *Pause.*

I didn't think so.

> *DOTTIE crosses to give GLADYS a hug.*

MARSHA

I would have gone in with you. Sonia was at work. One of us had to stay with Mama. She was only allowed into the outer room.

TERESA (VOICE OVER – REMOTE)

From there I saw you leave, found my way into the deserted room, climbed onto the bed and ran my hands over him, searching for a heart beat, which I knew was already still. I lay curled holding him within me and we flew one last time together above this place of cold choices, dancing brilliantly into each other's soul, time escaped, until I fell, spiraling down into his silent body.

> *FELIX holds MARSHA.*

FELIX

Marsha, love, please. Mama and Security James are going to be here any minute. You don't want her to see you crying.

> (addressing the group)

Now, how about drinks all around? Harry, maybe you've heard a good joke you could tell.

HELENE

(musingly)

Security James—such a handsome man.

DOTTIE

(beat)

I'll go get Trinka.

> *DOTTIE exits up the stairs.*
>
> *MUSIC: "DOTTIE and TRINKA'S Theme" plays as she exits.*
>
> *The living room LIGHTS fade as LIGHTS come up on TRINKA'S bedroom. TRINKA is sitting on her bed, her arms across her clenched knees. MUSIC fades.*

TRINKA

I hate them. Aunt Helene and Uncle Harry.

> *DOTTIE studies her little friend's face and decides not to respond; ignoring what TRINKA says, she looks at herself in the full-length mirror.*

DOTTIE

Do you think I am pretty?

TRINKA

You are beautiful.

DOTTIE

I still have one more year .

(sighing)

Security James... he seems so nice. But not the man I once...

TRINKA

(very curious)

Dottie, what man?

DOTTIE

A sliver of light... Now a shadow.

TRINKA

Do they know?

> *DOTTIE crosses to the doorway to make sure they will not be overheard then crosses back and sits close to TRINKA on the bed.*

DOTTIE

It happened so fast, we only had one moment. I was sitting in a bar, having a fizz and this guy... well you know me, I don't always think first... didn't ask... but he looked at me deep inside.

> *She stands up on the bed and her body begins to follow her words.*

We both stood up and met on the edge of the dance floor. We held onto each other, our bodies melted into one. He reached out to the hunger in me. In his eyes I saw myself whole, a woman in a woman's body shaking at his touch; so ready to love, be loved.

> *DOTTIE takes a deep breath.*

They came and said "wrong place, wrong group, leave now". He looked back at me and tried to smile. I could hear my heart break. It was a long time ago.

> *She sits back down next to TRINKA and they hug as DOTTIE wipes tears off her cheeks.*

Am I pretty enough for a good match? Next year I'll be 29 and they will start testing me... if I want to be part of the pool, be presented.

TRINKA

Do you still think of him?

DOTTIE

I try but cannot find him anymore in my dreams.

TRINKA

Dreams?

DOTTIE

I understand Gladys... she signed the contract to be alone because she became afraid; afraid there would be no one to love, no one who would save for her, easier not to ask.

TRINKA

I would save for you. I met a boy, Dottie.

DOTTIE

(quickly turning to look at Trinka, fearful for her young friend)

You are not permitted a boy yet!

TRINKA

(dreamily)

It was by accident... he had such slender fingers and they held mine for a minute. It was the first time, ever, I felt like I was "me", not just one of many. I was for the first time, outside of "all". Is that what it's like to dream?

DOTTIE

(worried)

What happened? Who was he?

TRINKA

(turning away from Dottie, hiding the truth)

Nothing happened. He just walked away.

DOTTIE, ending the discussion, gets up and goes back to the mirror.

DOTTIE

Will you go with me to the presentation if I decide?

TRINKA

Of course. But only if I can wear make-up. Please put some on me... please, Dottie.

DOTTIE

Ok, but not too much.

> *DOTTIE reaches under the bed for some makeup in her purse.*

Your grandmother will be here any minute.

> *TRINKA jumps up, laughs as DOTTIE seats her in front of the mirror then jumps up again.*

TRINKA

Music, we need some music.

> *She turns on her Wall. A world globe shows on the monitor, MUSIC: "The Wall" starts as we see the globe quickly replaced by the transmission of some sort of antigovernment demonstration. MUSIC out. A picture of AUNT SONIA is among the demonstrators. TRINKA gives a scream and runs out of the room. DOTTIE follows, the Wall continues to play. TRINKA screams as she crosses to her mother:*

Aunt Sonia; they have Aunt Sonia. Turn on the Wall. Turn on the WALL!

> *LIGHTS come up on the rest of the family. FELIX waves his hand over the monitor and the identical picture of AUNT SONIA and other demonstrators appears. Behind AUNT SONIA is a young boy.*

MARSHA & FELIX

Trinka, what is it? What's wrong?

TRINKA

The Wall! Turn on the Wall! Aunt Sonia—it's Aunt Sonia. I saw her.

MARSHA

Hush, child. Hush.

> *Everyone waits in various postures of fear for the image to appear. GUY'S face fills the Wall. On his image a TV film shows a line of people with linked arms demonstrating in front of what looks like a government building. They chant:*

DEMONSTRATORS

Alternative Systems. Alternative...

The sound abruptly stops. The camera pans over a few faces in close-up but too rapidly for any face to be absolutely clear. TRINKA points.

TRINKA

Dottie, look. There—look—next to the man by the guards. My boy... What will happen to him?

DOTTIE covers TRINKA'S mouth with her hand.

DOTTIE

Trinka, shhh, be quiet!

GUY'S face becomes the foreground. His uniform is darker.

GUY

The demonstration was crushed immediately. In order to protect all citizens' confidentiality, individual families will be notified as soon as the demonstrators have been coded. Some of you have had loved ones commit "minor offenses" in the past. And as a caring government we have been compassionate, not involving whole families; giving small penalties. But this time we cannot be so lenient. It is up to a family to persuade appropriate, law abiding conduct. For those of you affected by the law breakers in your family we will beam the picture of your loved one and list the point-fines as soon as the Ministry of Justice factualizes the information. These must be paid within 24 hours... and they will be quite heavy. Thank you.

The screen goes blank.

HELENE

(disgusted)

"Loved one"—indeed.

The others are frozen. Beat.

HARRY

Be quiet, please.

TRINKA

Daddy, was that Aunt Sonia?

FELIX

I couldn't tell.

MARSHA

It wasn't! It couldn't be. She wouldn't—not today, not now...

FELIX

Each year a struggle—now this! I'm getting old... tired.

TRINKA hugs FELIX.

TRINKA

Daddy, Daddy, please don't say you're old. Don't give up. Pretty soon I can help too. I promise. I will help any way I can.

FELIX

I know you will. It was Sonia, wasn't it, Marsha?

MARSHA exits into the kitchen.

MARSHA

No!

FELIX

Gladys?

GLADYS

I think so. What are we going to tell Mama?

The Wall comes on. GUY'S face fills the screen.

GUY

For those of you who have not met me yet, my name is Guy. I am your friend. I do regret this tragedy which has befallen you, particularly as it is your mother's birthday. However I am required to inform you that Sonia Hallick Lawrence, whom we have been actively tracking has been arrested as one of the leaders of today's demonstration. Her fine is set at 2000 points. She has now relinquished her entire next year's credit of 750 points, points given to all of our people under the age of 65. We are sorry that such a well known family has been trapped by one of its own members; especially knowing how long you have saved for each other. For Sonia's release we will still need an additional 1250 points.

> *MARSHA, at the kitchen door, starts to cry. GLADYS goes to her. DOTTIE goes to TRINKA. FELIX hides his head in his arms.*

HARRY

1,250 points! It's not fair!

GUY

I beg to differ. It's very reasonable. We strive to be reasonable.

(beat)

Hold one minute please... a message is reaching me... "Friends of Alternative Systems" have donated 150 points. I shall keep you continually informed as points come in. Please let me know of your own decision. Altogether, 1,100 are going to be needed in the next 24 hours. Please see what you can do.

(suddenly chatty)

Well, dear friends let's hear from you, and have a nice party for your mother.

> *The Wall goes dark.*

TRINKA

(to DOTTIE, whispering)

The boy from the job, I saw him. He was standing behind Aunt Sonia.

DOTTIE

Trinka, be quiet.

FELIX

Who is that dreadful man?

MARSHA

It's my fault. I just answered what they said was a census. Asking if a family wanted a coach. It was a census taking.

GLADYS

Why would we need a coach?

MARSHA

I thought it might help bring us closer.

FELIX

Marsha, you have let a stranger into our home.

HARRY

He was probably already here. We just did not notice.

GLADYS

What are we going to tell Mama? What are we going to do?

> DOTTIE has been listening at the door throughout the transmission.
>
> HELENE grabs HARRY'S hand and tries to yank him to his feet. He resists, briefly.

HELENE

Get up, Harry! We're going home.

HARRY

What? Going home? We just got here.

GLADYS

You can't leave. Marsha's gone to such trouble, such expense. You can't just leave.

HELENE starts to the door.

HELENE

Yes, we can and we're going to.

TRINKA blocks her.

TRINKA

What will Grandmamma say? Please, Aunt Helene. What will happen to Aunt Sonia?

HELENE

(leaning into TRINKA)

That's just it! Aunt Sonia is once again in trouble. This time it's very much worse than ever before. That means everyone in this family is now finally also a target. What group is Sonia with this time?

HARRY

Friends of Alternative Systems. People who want to go back to the old times.

FELIX

They advocate doing away with the point system.

HARRY

They also want to bring back disease.

HELENE

The only part of their platform that sounds sensible, if you ask me. If there were disease, people would just die. Make it easier. Harry, we are leaving, right now!!

MARSHA grabs HELENE'S arm, who shakes her off.

MARSHA

Helene, you've got to stay. Please. For Mama.

HELENE

It won't be for Mama. It'll be for Sonia, because you're going to make sure everyone in this room gives up something to get her fine paid. Well, we're not going to.

> *DOTTIE watches the door intently. The red light goes on over the door.*

DOTTIE

They're coming. Your mother's coming.

> *FELIX pulls out two chairs from the dining table and forces HELENE and HARRY to sit down.*

FELIX

Harry, Helene, sit down.

GLADYS

What are we going to tell Mama? What are we going to do?

> *HELENE and HARRY sit. MARSHA springs to command and hastily wipes her eyes.*

MARSHA

Nobody is to say anything! We'll switch the Wall on in our bedroom. Take turns receiving the count. Smile, everybody. It's Mama's birthday.

> *She rushes to the door. Everyone else freezes.*
>
> *The red lights flash around the door and the curtain falls.*

SCENE THREE

MUSIC: "Opening Music" starts in dark and plays briefly as the LIGHTS come up on TERESA and SECURITY JAMES waiting to be acknowledged. TERESA in her old fashioned wheelchair. SECURITY JAMES stands at attention with his hands on the handles of this "thing".

As the LIGHTS come up on her family TERESA has time to study their dismay and shock that she is in a wheelchair; something none of them have ever seen before.

TERESA allows a small, ironic smile to flick across her face. TERESA is a woman who will throughout Scene III move backward in time; starting out quite old, often enjoying a pose of age that has become comfortable. She's crotchety and withered like a gray leaf at the beginning. By the end, she has shed the cobwebs of time, age, and infirmity, and is, in spirit and in posture, the legend that legend made her.

TRINKA breaks through the crowd at the door and stops suddenly to study the wheelchair. The others take several steps and back away from TERESA. MUSIC fades.

TERESA

Is no one happy to see me?

TRINKA

Grandmamma! Grandmamma, you're here. I can finally touch you.

She is tentative about how to reach out to her grandmother, but does manage a big squeeze.

TERESA

Trinka, my beloved grandchild. I'm an old lady and should be treated like an eggshell.

HELENE

Does it cost extra points? The chair. Does it cost more?

HARRY

Helene, be quiet.

> *He embraces TERESA with a surge of emotion. HARRY tries to take the chair from SECURITY JAMES who quickly stops him.*

SECURITY JAMES

These are very rare machines. It took me a few times to understand how it works. So very rare.

EVERYONE (overlapping voices)

What do you call it? Does it hurt? Happy Birthday, Mama.

HARRY

Show me how to push this thing. I want to bring Teresa into the room.

> *They bend over at the back of the chair and adjust something. Together they push TERESA into the center of the room and turn the chair to face the audience. MARSHA is visibly shaken.*

MARSHA

Why were we not informed? What happened? Security James, why were we not told?

SECURITY JAMES

The points were already calculated and the release form approved. We thought it best you celebrate this birthday as planned. We all saw how much effort you had put into getting ready to celebrate.

DOTTIE

Teresa, what happened?

TERESA

My legs defeat me.

DOTTIE

Are you comfortable in that thing?

TERESA

It's called a wheelchair. I remember them from long ago. Old people in chairs. Yes, we had them. Had both actually; old people and wheelchairs.

> *Everyone suddenly breaks apart and hugs and touches her. For one brief moment, only love, all the love potential in any family reunion is real and right. HELENE is last; she holds her mother in a long embrace and bursts into tears.*

Child. Child. Tears on my birthday?

HELENE

I'm so glad to see you!

> *TERESA holds HELENE gently.*

TERESA

So you moved out of the city to forget me?

HELENE

Oh, Mama!

TERESA

I know you so well... I am very glad to see you. I was not sure you would come.

> *She embraces HELENE who, crying, goes to HARRY; he holds her.*

> *DOTTIE, who has been hiding the real flower behind her back, pulls it out and presents it to TERESA. TERESA accepts it with a grateful nod.*

A flower. A real flower. Dottie, what a marvelous gift for me. This will be the most wonderful of all my birthdays.

> *DOTTIE hugs TERESA.*

DOTTIE

I hope so. I do hope so.

TERESA

Thank you, Dottie.

> *TRINKA sits on the floor next to her grandmother; HARRY goes upstairs.*

MARSHA

Security James—how awful! None of us have said thank you for the extra work you must have done. Bringing Mama in this thing.

> *SECURITY JAMES gives a slight nod of his head.*

> *FELIX positions himself behind MARSHA and SECURITY JAMES.*

SECURITY JAMES

(sotto voce)

I've been informed, you know.

FELIX

We know. We're taking turns checking on the wall in our bedroom. We don't want Mama to worry; spoil her party. Please don't say anything.

> *HARRY returns and crosses to the group.*

HARRY

(sotto voce)

Nothing's changed. 1096 to pay off the charges.

> *He moves toward the bar. TERESA calls to SECURITY JAMES.*

TERESA

I think I need a cup of tea...

TRINKA

I'll do it.

TERESA

Yes, that will be fine.

> *TRINKA rushes to the kitchen.*

Where's Sonia? Is she coming? Why is she late?

GLADYS

Of course she's coming; she's just delayed.

TERESA

(suddenly querulous)

I need some tea.

HARRY

Trinka's getting it, Mama.

TERESA

Security James, you always make my tea perfectly. You always make my tea on Sundays.

SECURITY JAMES

Teresa, you are with your family.

> TRINKA *comes back into the room from the kitchen carrying a cup.*

TRINKA

Grandmamma, we like to do things for you.

MARSHA

Security James, would you like a drink? Tea? Coffee?

> GLADYS *exits to check the monitor.*

SECURITY JAMES

Nothing, thank you.

> HELENE *slides up to* SECURITY JAMES.

HELENE

It's a party, Security James. Just this once you could have a drink.

SECURITY JAMES

Why, thank you. A drink would be just fine. Maybe one of those oxygen fizzes.

> *SECURITY JAMES and FELIX cross to the bar to get the drink. FELIX fixes the drink.*

TRINKA

How is it, Grandmamma?

TERESA

It's perfect, child, perfect.

TRINKA

It's not too hot?

HELENE

Last year you burned your lip, so be careful.

TERESA

I said it was perfect. Where did you say Sonia was? Helene, what a pretty dress. Where are my grandsons?

> *HELENE looks to HARRY. He shrugs and turns his back leaving her flustered.*

HELENE

Well, Mama, they really wanted to come, but... uh... they're...

TERESA

Busy! They are always busy, even though for elders' birthdays everyone is given time. The young never have time. The old, too much.

TRINKA

But Grandmother, the rest of us are all here. Aren't we enough?

> *TERESA pats TRINKA.*

TERESA

Of course, child. It's nice for me to know that you come such a long distance so that I can see you.

TRINKA

Oh, Grandmamma. It's so I can see you.

TERESA

Others don't even come a much shorter distance.

> *GLADYS enters the room. Everyone clusters around GLADYS as far as possible from TERESA so as not to be overheard. GLADYS gives a negative shake of her head.*

> *SECURITY JAMES notices the interaction, puts down his drink and calls out to TERESA.*

SECURITY JAMES

You're comfortable, Teresa? Would you like a little pillow behind your back?

> *TERESA gives a dismissive negative wave of her hand.*

> *Until the family moves towards the dining area to sit down, they will begin to cluster into various groups, break apart, and reform. TERESA remains facing the audience throughout these exchanges. The LIGHTS will spotlight on a group with audible dialogue, and dim only to brighten momentarily somewhere else on another group.*

> *The LIGHTS brighten on the dining area. GLADYS, DOTTIE and HARRY are momentarily heard.*

GLADYS

(sotto voce)

The count is still the same. 1096 to get Sonia here.

DOTTIE

What are we going to do?

GLADYS

Sonia, Sonia, so like Mama. I wasn't going on a vacation anyway... it was really a weight control spa. Maybe if I were slimmer I would meet a man... just as a companion of course. I would never break the law... even a fat man would be nice, I think... Oh well—it can wait... It costs 100 points. Sonia can have them.

> *MARSHA gives GLADYS a hug. HARRY crosses to the dining area. He studies the table. GLADYS goes upstairs. SECURITY JAMES, who has been talking to MARSHA and FELIX, responds to a buzz on his neck computer chip.*

SECURITY JAMES

Recent donations: 100, oh, here's another 100 from the public, 896 still needed to get your sister here.

MARSHA

I wish I had some savings to give Sonia...

SECURITY JAMES

(gently)

Mother Hallick perhaps you need to reconsider. You've done all you can for a long time. Perhaps it's time to make a decision—a different one. You will never have any savings the way you are going.

MARSHA

I can't make THAT decision.

> *She waves in the direction of the birthday table.*

I need this. I need to believe that we love each other.

SECURITY JAMES

(to FELIX)

Perhaps, you'll have to make the decision for her.

MARSHA

No!!!

> *FELIX hugs MARSHA.*

*GLADYS reenters, crosses first to the kitchen, confers with
DOTTIE briefly, then crosses to dining area. LIGHTS up on
TRINKA and TERESA. TRINKA sits on the floor next to her
grandmother and speaks in a whisper.*

TRINKA

Mama told me about the children and the doorway people.

(TERESA looks shocked)

Grandmother, what was in the last stadium?

TERESA

Trinka, child, leave the past alone. Enjoy what you have today.

(TRINKA raises her voice)

TRINKA

Please, I have to know.

(HARRY overhears)

HARRY

(a bit "high")

Have to know what?

(raising his voice)

Have to know what?

FELIX

Lower your voice, Harry. You are in my home.

SECURITY JAMES

Have to know what?

TERESA

About this chair. If it's comfortable.

*FELIX and SECURITY JAMES drift towards the table leaving
TRINKA, TERESA, HARRY and HELENE. MARSHA, DOTTIE and
GLADYS are quietly in the kitchen area.*

DOTTIE

Marsha, do you like Trinka's make-up?

MARSHA

(absently)

It's all right.

GLADYS

She's a bit young. But pretty. And thin. Thin is good.

Lights up on HARRY and HELENE.

HELENE

We should go–they are only going to ask us to give more points.

HARRY

Helene, she's your sister... Don't you care?

HELENE

No, Harry, I don't. I don't care about any of them. It's too expensive to care for ANY of them... And what about our sons? Why should we deprive our sons?

HARRY

You think they would care about us? They way you've brought them up?

HELENE punches him on the arm. He shrugs her off.

You think they would give a damn about saving us... Flowers... FLOWERS!

HELENE tugs at him, she does not want this story told.

HARRY almost beside himself at the memory which has been eating him for years:

FLOWERS, BEAUTIFUL, LIVING, FLOWERS!!!

MUSIC: "HARRY'S Flowers" starts here.

LIGHTS up on TERESA and TRINKA. HARRY speaks at TRINKA.

HARRY (CONT.)

The last stadium was filled with flowers. Thousands of flowers. All kinds. All colors. It was so beautiful. It was so beautiful. I was one of the children in the children's stadium... We could see the flowers wilt and die. I remember the frost on my toes before I was given the pair of shoes. After all the families had left, we were ordered to stay; wait, wonder if any one of us would be among the few chosen. It snowed on us. I took off Sonia's shoes and held them up so you would find me.

> (to TERESA)

And you came. One stadium step at a time. At the bottom you stopped, gave the contract to the guard. He led you to me.

> (kneeling next to TERESA)

You knelt down, put your arms around me, lifted me and carried me out of the children's stadium. I turned and waved at the little girl whose hand I had been holding. You took me home to your garden of family and flowers. And to my first love, Marsha.

> *MUSIC ends.*

> *HELENE screams at HARRY as she gets out of the chair and heads for the door.*

HELENE

That does it. I'm leaving! It has always been Marsha. You turned your back on me years ago.

> *HARRY moves towards HELENE. He has grown into a powerful man.*

HARRY

What noise your ancient anger makes, raining pain on me as over the years I have tried to reach you. Be quiet, woman, be silent. Put your old jealousy to rest. Let me love you. I loved your sister as a child, but for you I have been a loving husband and friend. It is you who turns away.

> *HARRY reaches out a hand to brush HELENE'S hair.*

HELENE
(confused, trying to adjust to her inner turmoil)

You might love me?

HARRY

I have tried but through your anger you never hear me.

HELENE twirls in her dress.

HELENE
(ready to risk it all)

Am I pretty to you, Harry?

HARRY

Yes.

They embrace with intensity. The LIGHTS go dark as they walk together to the bar.

The LIGHTS come up on TERESA and TRINKA. They are very private in a corner and not easily seen by others.

TRINKA

The story, Grandmamma. Tell me the story like you told me when I was little. I need to hear it.

TERESA looks at TRINKA very carefully.

TERESA

Trinka, child. You have to look ahead.

TRINKA

Please tell me.

TERESA

I never knew if you believed my stories. What if they never were the way I told them?

TRINKA

I know they were real, not fantasies. Please, Grandmamma. One more time. Tell me one more time. I want to hear it from you. As I did as a child.

TERESA

Where should I start?

TRINKA

Please, the way you always do. It starts, once upon a time...

MARSHA has crossed to the kitchen.

MARSHA

We really have to eat.

HARRY comes back into the room and nods at SECURITY JAMES before sitting down. Everyone else sits down. SECURITY JAMES remains standing, positioning himself between the table and the kitchen. SECURITY JAMES listens to his neck implant.

SECURITY JAMES

Someone just donated 146 points to Sonia.

The LIGHTS go down on the group at the table as they freeze. It is only after everyone is seated that the LIGHTS come up on TRINKA and TERESA.

TRINKA

Once upon a time...

TERESA

The change came very quickly. Almost overnight, the laws changed. Everything and everyone that cost but did not produce were considered a luxury—old people, pets, birds in cages and little things of great beauty, like flowers. There were no severe shortages but the planners thought everyone would agree to give up those things that they themselves did not treasure: people and things that had no value to them. And most did agree.

TRINKA

Grandmother, that's not the way to tell the story.

TERESA

How is it told?

TRINKA

You ran, you ran into the forest. When they said all the dogs, cats, and birds in their cages had to be given up, you ran with your little dog and hid in the forest.

TERESA

And the flowers.

TRINKA

That took too much water. You picked all the flowers.

TERESA

I picked all of them. All the fields I passed. All the flowers I could carry—I knew there would be no more allowed to grow just for their beauty. A year later, the point system came in.

TRINKA

Grandmother... go on!

TERESA

He and I hid for three days in the field at the edge of the forest. He only left my side once—to chase a butterfly. He slept with his head on my knee. I held him and tried to explain—to apologize for what was going to happen. I knew he would be found. On the third day, when I heard them... he heard them too. He whimpered once, very softly, and I fed him the pills. He licked my hand. I held him, talked to him until it was over. He was safe. When the guards found us, I was still holding him. They arrested me... but they couldn't hurt him. He was safe.

TRINKA

And...

TERESA

The newspapers liked the story, made much of it. Suddenly, everyone was embarrassed. They let me go. After all, I had four daughters. And Harry, my adopted beloved son. That was a long time ago.

TRINKA

Grandmamma, I want to give you a present.

TERESA

Child, you shouldn't buy me anything. You have to keep your points. You have to learn to save.

TRINKA

I didn't buy it. Someone a boy... he was so beautiful Grandmamma, he gave it to me for you. He said you would want it.

> *TRINKA stands up, quickly goes to her room, gets the memory disk from under the bed pillow, studies it knowing she is about to commit a crime, places it in her skirt pocket, leaves the room and crosses back to her grandmother in the wheelchair.*

He said it was a birthday present for you, from many others, who remember you. Who want to hear you tell your story. Who are waiting to hear you tell your story.

> *TRINKA removes the illegal memory disk from her skirt pocket and places it in TERESA'S outstretched hands. TERESA begins to sob.*

> *MARSHA calls to TRINKA from the dining room:*

MARSHA

Trinka, come.

SECURITY JAMES

I'll go get them.

> *He moves towards the secluded place where TERESA and TRINKA are huddled.*

> *SECURITY JAMES, unnoticed, observes them. He enters the area.*

TERESA

My disk.

TRINKA

It belongs to you.

MARSHA crosses into the room. SECURITY JAMES is transfixed, staring at the object in TERESA'S hands.

TERESA

My disk. For years, I have wanted to see it one more time... to be able to look at a time, now past as I am past.

MARSHA

(stunned and afraid)

Trinka, what have you done?!

SECURITY JAMES

All the disks were confiscated years ago. Where did you get this? I have to report this. This is a crime!

The entire group has left the dining room and is in the living room.

TERESA

(to SECURITY JAMES)

Please, leave her alone. She gave me the greatest gift of all—to live so long and never be allowed to see an old snapshot, an old tape, a beloved face or relive a beautiful day.

SECURITY JAMES moves threateningly toward TRINKA.

SECURITY JAMES

Trinka, I insist. Where did you get it?

TRINKA

(backing away from him)

I've had it for years... I found it when we moved a long time ago.

GLADYS

Oh my god, the disk!

SECURITY JAMES

Trinka, you know that is not true. You know I know that is not true.
We all are trained to spot illegal traffickers. That boy... we had
been watching him... did you accept this from him? Did you accept
this from him? He has been taken away. You have committed a
crime. I have to report you.

> *His hands shake as he picks up the remote. He is suddenly*
> *uncertain as to what to do with it: to report it or not.*

> *FELIX moves between TRINKA and SECURITY JAMES barely*
> *able to control his anger.*

FELIX

Leave my daughter alone.

HARRY

Security James, you're our friend... Teresa's guardian. It's a party, a
birthday party. Today—just once, you can look the other way.

HELENE

The disk. The family legend, family curse.

> *HARRY grasps HELENE'S arm.*

HARRY

Helene, stop it, stop!

> *TERESA struggles to get out of the chair. Though she is very*
> *weak, she shakes off HARRY'S attempt to help her. Her first*
> *steps are uncertain but she begins to gain strength as she*
> *moves towards the Wall and places the disk on the player.*
> *Projected on the Wall is a picture of a young woman sitting in*
> *a field of flowers. A little dog is running around her. It is a*
> *lengthier series of the images TRINKA played in Scene I. The*
> *last image is of TERESA, as a young woman, holding the dog*
> *as she pets him and feeds him the pills. The picture freezes.*

TERESA

I have longed to see this one picture again. Do you see such great harm, Security James?

SECURITY JAMES

It is forbidden.

TERESA

Do you know why?

SECURITY JAMES

It is best not to question. It makes it easier to live without memory of that time.

TERESA

Do you really believe we have forgotten?

SECURITY JAMES

No one Trinka's age should have her head filled with dangerous nonsense.

> *SECURITY JAMES yanks the disk/globe out of the player and the screen goes blank.*

That time is gone, cannot ever be again. We will make certain those times will not come again. Better they be forgotten.

TERESA

Memory isn't dangerous the way you think, Security James. It wasn't only the flowers and the bright birds—it is that you took chance and God away. When you took smaller living things away, you killed part of the God you left in place. You were too smart to take God away, just pieces of one's faith.

SECURITY JAMES
(with a raised voice)

Teresa, there was no room for the things you loved. No room, no room for pets or flowers or old people.

TERESA

Who would teach the next generation and the ones that came after love and compassion for smaller things, bright things, dependent people, not strong people but weak?

SECURITY JAMES

There was no room. There is NO room.

TERESA

We all must live until others choose a time for us to go.

MARSHA

Mama, don't.

TERESA

It was better to die another way. Not always gracefully but knowing there were swallows migrating, flowers growing, and possibly a boy to love. I always loved chance and you finally took chance away.

HELENE

(desperate)

Security James, please don't listen. She doesn't know what she's saying.

HARRY

Of course she does.

GUY appears on the Wall; no longer the family's friend, now the ruler of society.

GUY

It is necessary for me to take Trinka's transgression to The Committee. I will announce the decision as it is finalized.

GUY fades from the screen. SECURITY JAMES moves toward TRINKA. FELIX moves toward SECURITY JAMES.

FELIX

This is my flesh, this is my blood. In her, my child, I remember the dawn of her first step, and through her a different time, when all children were mine to hold and pray over, protect their laughter running like a river of happiness towards the sky. This is my child. You touch her, you take her, I am nothing but loss, nowhere to look but into my own empty heart. You touch my child, I will see you-

MARSHA

(breaks down)

All the years, years of trying to keep a balance.

TRINKA

I am sorry Mama, I did not mean to make you sad. I just wanted to know about the past. Now I know. It really was what Grandmamma told me long ago... I'm really tired. I want to lie down.

TERESA

Of course, rest. It will all be fine. Come give me a hug.

> *TERESA and TRINKA hug. TRINKA starts to her room. Marsha goes with TRINKA to the staircase and watches her as she takes each step towards her bedroom. FELIX moves aggressively towards SECURITY JAMES who backs away from him. HELENE screams at TRINKA'S back.*

HELENE

You've finally done it! You and Sonia. Bad enough we've always been watched so closely—more than any other family.

> *Turning to HARRY.*

All the years my sons were growing up, I was afraid they'd make a mistake. I was afraid they'd be like Mama or Sonia

> *Turning to MARSHA.*

and now Trinka. It's all gone anyway.

TERESA

Is that why you never included me in their lives. You were afraid I would tell them of how it once was? Helene, each year when they come to tell me I have another one, I weep. I know there are things you want for yourself. And Marsha, loving daughter, you would keep me until I am a hundred... but to what purpose? It is time to finish.

MARSHA

Please, Mama. Please don't.

TERESA

What joy can there be for me at the end of my life, if there is no joy for you, my children?

> Unsteady on her feet, TERESA beckons HARRY to her and commands he answer her.

Now, you better tell me about Sonia.

HARRY

Sonia?

TERESA

You can do better than that, Harry. She's in trouble, isn't she?

HARRY

Trouble? What kind of trouble?

TERESA

(insistent)

I trust you, Harry, to answer me right now. Where is Sonia? What has happened to Sonia?

HARRY

She's been arrested.

TERESA

Has she been harmed?

HARRY

Arrested as the leader of a demonstration today. No.

TERESA

For my birthday. Sonia, my youngest child. The day I left for the
forest, she followed me. My little one, she fell and started to cry.
We went back. I gave her to Marsha to hold. In her little, high, baby
voice she said she would never forget. She never did. Can I see her?

FELIX

Yes, Mama.

TERESA

You too have been a gift to this family. I want you to know that by
giving Marsha the baby girl she so wanted, you earned my love. You
too have been a remarkable son. You will have to hold Marsha and
Trinka very close. I would like to see Sonia. Is it possible?

HARRY

Yes, I'll see to it.

HELENE

We will see to it.

TERESA

What does Sonia need?

FELIX

Sonia needs 750 points.

TERESA

My family has already guaranteed that amount for my birthday.
Security James, please inform The Committee that I wish my
daughter Sonia be given these and that she be released.

SECURITY JAMES

You are certain? Once made there is no withdrawing such a decision.

TERESA

Of course, I am certain.

> *SECURITY JAMES touches his neck computer a few times,*
> *sending some signal and finally nods consent.*

I taught you memories that were mine from a different time. In that way, it seems I did not serve you well. I have, in fact, made your lives more difficult.

> *One by one she embraces her family.*

I leave you knowing that you will, as you must, care for each other. As you grow older, your lives will depend on the love you gave each other. You have taught me that love comes back many times.

> (to MARSHA)

You worry too much. They say it is over quickly. Everything done most gently.

> *TRINKA stands in her bedroom doorway to listen to her family*
> *quarrel. GUY becomes visible on her's and the central monitor.*

GUY

We have very good news. We will be releasing Sonia to you very shortly. And our decision for Trinka is also good news: 3 years in re-orientation. We are showing such sensitivity because she will then be 18 and still be able to be part of the pool. We believe she can be salvaged.

> *The family is stunned.*

SECURITY JAMES

This is too harsh!!!

> *The LIGHTS go dark on the family and come up on TRINKA'S*
> *room. MUSIC: "TRINKA'S Theme" starts.*
>
> *TRINKA, visible to the audience, sits at her small dressing table*
> *writing a short message on a piece of paper; stands up,*
> *slowly, takes a pill from a vial on her nightstand and puts it*
> *into her mouth. She lies down on her bed. MUSIC fades.*
>
> *LIGHTS come up on the family.*

SECURITY JAMES (CONT.)

That is too harsh.

(to GUY on the Wall)

That is too harsh. She is just a child... I will get the disk. Bring it back to you to destroy... Please... This is MY family. This young girl is like my own child. I love her.

GUY

We must make an example because she is a child... Security James you are a "Security". You must follow orders. In this case, since you say this is your "family", you have failed to keep the proper distance. Your failure, Security James, has allowed The Committee to identify the flaws in Phase One: the human attachment will be removed in Phase Two. Security James, you are dismissed from service. My decisions are final.

FELIX

(appealing to GUY)

Take me, take me, take me. How can you take all my tomorrows? How can you shatter my very soul, leave my spirit frozen in this unforgiving place. Take me. Take my broken moment of self and leave my child safe.

MUSIC: "TRINKA'S Theme" plays.

MARSHA

(a sudden shudder)

MARSHA runs out of the room and up the steps.

LIGHTS fade on FELIX and the family.

Trinka, baby. Trinka? Where are you? I know you're in your room. Come out, come out, come to your mother.

MARSHA enters the bedroom, looks down at TRINKA and touches TRINKA'S body. She sinks onto the bed, lifts TRINKA into her arms and cradles her lifeless body.

MARSHA (CONT.)

Trinka, wake up, Trinka, wake up. Sweet pea, wake up.

> *MARSHA begins to keen, her moaning growing louder. FELIX runs up the stairs to MARSHA'S side.. MARSHA continues to rock TRINKA.*

(rocking Trinka's body)

Trinka baby, do not leave me. Do not leave me.

> *MARSHA'S sobs fill the entire room. They fade to low moans as she continues to rock the body.*

> *FELIX takes a note from TRINKA'S lifeless hand, descends the steps, crosses to TERESA and hands her TRINKA'S note. MUSIC fades. FELIX quickly crosses back to TRINKA'S bedroom and leans over MARSHA to comfort her. LIGHTS fade on everyone on stage except TERESA who is now center stage.*

TERESA

Oh, Trinka, this was to be my last birthday. I had already seen the end, was an observer to my last counting of points…was eager to leave and be with my love, not to stay here crushed by your sacrifice, your parents' bitter weeping.

Beloved grandchild, I will try, carrying you in my heart every day.

You, careless soldier, soulless face on a monitor with no memory of times of choice, a family with elders, a bird's song or a flower's remarkable beauty. You have caused another gentle spirit to die.

Trinka, beloved grandchild, I will do as you ask. Live to tell my story yet another year and keep memory alive. Good night my beautiful little one.

Now you can sleep… Now you are free to dream.

> *The curtain falls. MUSIC: "TRINKA'S Theme" plays out.*

THE END.

BIOGRAPHY

Tania Wisbar was born in Berlin, Germany to mother, Eva Theresa Krojanker Wysbar and father, Franz Paul Wysbar, renowned German film and TV director and creator of The Fireside Theater, an classic American television anthology series in the 1950's.

Tania has spent her life around films and theater, starting with her visits to her father's film sets and reading script material for him.

She attended Mills College in California receiving a degree in Theater Arts and in the years following graduation attended the Pasadena Playhouse, the Provincetown Playhouse in Massachusetts and the Cleveland Playhouse.

Returning to education, Tania received a Master's Degree in Speech Pathology.

Recruited by the Los Angeles County Superintendent's office to join a small group of specialists to introduce autistic children into public education settings, Tania made a very early teacher training film about these children entitled "In A World Alone".

Soon after this, Tania started her own specialized program for developmentally delayed or disabled infants and adults.

In its 30 years of operation, her agency, Behavior, Education and Learning Institute (B.E.L.I.), has provided over a million hours of service to families on the east side of Los Angeles with children between 18 and 36 months and adults between the ages of 23 to 60 years of age.

Always interested in writing, Tania and her husband, John Francis Mahoney, (deceased in 2006), moved to a small beach town south of San Diego and started a newspaper which they owned for 14 years.

During these years Tania served as editor and journalist for the newspaper.

In 2010 Tania finished the stage play "The Birthday Present 2050" after a 10 year absence from the material.

The play ran for 6 weeks at the Skylight Theater in Los Angeles in 2011 to positive reviews.

It is now available for performance by professional and amateur theater companies and can also be acquired as an audio play.

Please contact: birthdaypresent2050@argyleroadproductions.com

REVIEWS

A cult classic in the making.

—L.A. NEWS

Stories about dystopian societies often risk seeming contrived, but playwright Tania Wisbar's beautifully detailed and elegiac tale depicts a world that might believably exist, say, 100 years after a Nazi takeover. In the future, poverty and disease have been eliminated, but the world is instead organized on entirely practical lines, with your right to survive being decided by the number of "points" you earn every year. On the 75th birthday of family matriarch Teresa (Salome Jens), her devoted daughter Marsha (Elyssa Davalos) thinks she has collected enough points from her two sisters and family to allow Teresa to live another year. More than just being the emotional center of her clan, Teresa is one of the last living rebels who recalls life before the odious new order came to pass. Marsha's hopes are threatened when unexpected complications up the fee for Teresa's right to life. In director Jonathan Sanger's beautifully melancholy staging, what could be a mechanical exercise in high-concept plotting becomes a wistful tale of how easy it would be to purge memory of the past from the world. Sanger's smoothly executed production boasts many rich details: Set designer Kis Knekt's calculatedly sterile living room is replete with decorative video screens that show 1984esque messages from the genially sinister bureaucrat (Jeffrey Doornbos) who oversees the family's doings. Knekt's set, in conjunction with composer Karen Martin's eerie incidental music, crafts a world that's just plain crazy. The ensemble work is just as assured. Apart from Jens' powerful turn as the ferociously nonconforming grandmother, Davalos' complex performance as Marsha is exceptional: Her character is seemingly an upbeat chirper, but her good mood is so clearly artificial, it seems as though she's always about to weep. Also engaging in supporting roles are Katrina Lenk, as Marsha's venomously selfish younger sister, and Demetrius Grosse, as a guilt-haunted security agent.

—L.A. WEEKLY THEATER CRITICS
Thursday, Mar 24 2011

This remarkable plays draws upon our past, with echoes of Kafka and Orwell, while offering a vivid, frightening glimpse of our future. But mostly it tells us about who we are today, citizens of a society where anything can become a commodity – even relationships, even time. The language is poetic, but it builds to a haunting and powerful finale. The Birthday Present 2050 makes us look at as simple a thing as a bouquet of flowers with renewed appreciation.

—ERIK HANSEN
Artist-in-Residence, University of New Orleans

Like the classics of dystopian literature–think *Farenheit 451* by Ray Bradbury, *A Clockwork Orange* by Anthony Burgess, and more recently, *The Hunger Games* by Suzanne Collins, *The Birthday Present 2050* is a dystopian play by Tania Wisbar that takes a dark look at a disturbing contemporary trend and magnifies it under future totalitarian conditions. *The Birthday Present 2050* takes place in a society in which only people and things considered "productive" are assured existence; It posits a future society perfect and brutal, where citizens must choose each year between extending the life of an aging loved one, or accumulating more comfort for "the family" based on an earned point system. The story begs the reader– What would you choose? What makes it so unique and chilling is the entire play is set around the family dinner table, a quaint anachronism in the ordered, unsentimental future of 2050. And unlike its cousins in literature, *the Birthday Present 2050* is a play–a distilled vision of a disturbing world that goes to the heart of what we value as humans.

—KATHERINE M. STULBERG
Former Director, San Luis Obispo County Arts Council

www.ingramcontent.com/pod-product-compliance
Lightning Source LLC
Chambersburg PA
CBHW060133260626
47160CB00005B/2097